MUSEUMS

Susan C. Barto

THIRD EDITION

©opyright 1999, 2008, 2013 by Susan C. Barto

Library of Congress Control Number: 99-72405

ISBN-10: 0-9712516-2-2
ISBN-13: 9780971251625

Gary Drury's Publishing™

Kentucky

Produced in The United States of America.

DEDICATION

MY BELOVED HUSBAND,
and MY SON BILL.

CONTENTS

Barbara

The essence of Barbara was like a flickering candle flame on a windy night. She was such a joyous spirit, trying to carry others along on her tide of optimism. Once, although not at that time a new mother herself, she hosted a party for all the young mothers and the children on her block so that they could meet and have kindred spirits to help each other. Her lot with men over the course of her life was, with few exceptions, terrible. Her first husband died of leukemia after a long illness during which she had nursed him. He died right before Christmas, and she remembered that the worst time had been one evening when she came home cold and weary with the tree and the children's presents and almost didn't have the heart to carry them all into the house (now bereft of her husband's presence) to say nothing of setting it all up for the children. But, of course, she managed as she always did, and the children had their Christmas.

I first met Barbara in the hospital where I was scheduled to have a gall bladder operation. She was a dear friend of mutual friends, and she walked into my room bearing a smile to warm the hearts of snowmen. She announced that she was in the hospital awaiting an operation to remove her spleen, but that her blood count had to be just right, so at the present time she had been in the hospital for a month. She informed me that she had a closet in her room brimming with liquor and cheese and crackers, and that even some of the nurses joined in her cocktail hour, not to mention her rapidly changing roommates. She was so full of kindness for me and the other patients on the floor that no one would ever have guessed how serious her own condition was. She was an angel of cheer on the floor and said it was due to the fact that a friend who worked in the hospital brought her strong cup of coffee at dawn since breakfast wasn't served until 8:00. She was to remain in the hospital for nearly a month after I had returned home. She did finally have her operation, and a long recuperation period followed when her beautiful face was swollen from the Cortisone drugs she was forced to take. She never complained, and both of us were to view that time in the hospital as the beginning of a special friendship.

Barbara had two children from her first marriage, Jeannie and Michael. Michael was a brilliant young man with, unfortunately, severe emotional problems. Jeannie was a bright, sunny spirit; exactly the kind of beautiful, individual you would expect from a mother like Barbara. Barbara had will power like steel. She hypnotized herself so that she never ate sweets at any time because she claimed to have been a chubby child. When I knew her she was as slender as a flower stem, and Jeannie said that as much as she adored Barbara, she had always wanted a big motherly type with huge blossoms. Once when coffee prices zoomed to almost $5 a pound, Barbara hypnotized herself so that she only drank tea until the price came down. Barbara had an uncontrollable weakness about only one thing - drink. Barbara was an alcoholic; unfortunately her renown will power couldn't help her when it came to liquor. She was Jekyll and Hyde—like regarding her behavior when she was drinking and when she wasn't. The alcohol in some ways intensified her essence, and she was more loving and more of a crusader when she was drunk than when sober.

She had always been involved in politics, as we were at that time, and after drinking she was known to make many a midnight telephone call sometimes to the White House itself to proport her views on the current hot issue. She also made midnight telephone calls on behalf of her friends. She once called a close, mutual political ally of ours a 'horse's ass' with great justification, but to my dismay, nevertheless. Once following a misguided impulse she telephoned the Senator for whom I was a Legislative Aide on a day when he had falsely chastised me. This helpful gesture almost cost me my job, but I never had the heart to tell her. She, as usual, had meant well. This particular contretemps with the Senator and me was about who should be our next governor on the general election ballot since this was just before the primary. I was fiercely attempting to stay neutral so as not to defy the Senator by publicly supporting my candidate. A political enemy of mine had caused the Senator to believe that I was handing out literature for my candidate and displaying his bumper stickers on my car. When Barbara heard this her sense of humor again took over, and that night when we went out to the car to join her and her husband for dinner my candidate's bumper stickers were plastered all over our car. How she managed that without our knowing I'll never know, but it was very Barbara.

When I met Barbara in the hospital she was married or trying to escape from a disastrous marriage to a local rather prominent realtor. They had met while he was still involved in a troubled marriage, and he subsequently divorced, and they married. A mistake almost from the first moment. Their fights were legendary, even including an incident when he locked her out one cold, wet evening; and she almost ended up with pneumonia. He hurt Jeannie severely when he wouldn't allow her to call him Dad. He claimed that he wasn't her father. I never heard good news about this marriage, and mercifully, it was over before I even became friends with her. Barbara was a close friend of two political friends of ours, Dick and Peggy, who were having problems within their own marriage. Peggy's solution to many of their arguments was to tell Dick to go over and see Barbara. It was almost as if she were throwing them together, yet when the two of them exploded like a comet she was the one who was surprised. Barbara and Dick's love, like Barbara's life, streaked across the sky like a meteor shower. When my husband and I first saw Dick and Barbara appearing together at social functions we were a little puzzled but confused as to what it signified. Since they were obviously not sneaking around, we assumed that Peggy knew, and it was a kind of friendship thing. However, it soon became apparent that this was not the case because Barbara and Dick fell so deeply in love that they didn't trouble to hide it any longer. For both it was the first relationship in their lives where each was the most important person in the other's life. They buoyed and brightened each other's days. They couldn't stop telling

11

everyone with whom they came in contact how they felt about each other, how lucky they were, and how they never expected to have this happen to them. When the divorce was final, and they finally married, the romance just continued and even intensified. They were so passionate about each other that they tried to share their love and joy with everyone. Barbara was always inviting the lonely to all her holiday dinners as well as giving impromptu dinners just because she felt someone needed her.

Once a neighbor of Barbara's, who was a Vietnamese refugee as were her husband and children, lost her husband. This fell at the same time as my birthday, and Barbara had invited me to join her at the Summit Art Center where she was herself involved as an artist. The Summit Art Center was having a luncheon and fashion show, and my invitation was her birthday present to me. Barbara asked me whether I would mind if she brought along her recently widowed friend. I, of course , said that I wouldn't mind, but I had grave reservations because I felt that the outing might increase the new widow's grief. My instincts were wrong, and Barbara's gesture turned out to be a healthy gust of life to the young woman. We sat in the auditorium of the Summit Art Center and were each given box lunches and something to drink. While we nibbled on our lunches the fashion show was going on. Barbara's friend seemed to really enjoy the fashions, even laughing at some of the more extreme ones. After the fashion show door prizes were awarded, and Barbara won a little painting of a Spring landscape, which she promptly gave to me for my birthday present. She even tried to trade it for a cat painting, since I collected cats, but although she wasn't successful in this, I was more than delighted with the painting I had. After the fashion show we three went to Barbara's house, and Barbara's friend said that this had been her first outing and how wonderful it had been. Over coffee and cake we three were able to discuss the horror of her experience in a way we wouldn't have been able to do without the excursion of the fashion show.

Barbara had worked all her life mostly out of necessity, and she had an important position in an advertising firm in the art department. Her marriage to Dick came about at a time when most of us were going back to work — delighted to get away from the house and child raising at last. Barbara, no longer under the financial necessity of working, happily resigned her job, and she commenced painting full-time laughing to us especially on Sunday nights,

"Tomorrow morning when I'm sipping my second cup of coffee and contemplating what I'm going to paint today you'll all be driving to work."

Staying home, painting, and cooking for Dick seemed to make Barbara happier than she'd ever been. Hers was the place I'd go to on my way home from work on a disappointing day, and though I would arrive frustrated and worn, I was revitalized by the time I was ready to leave. Barbara loved holidays, events, and parties. She threw herself into the Bicentennial with a feverish intensity — sewing all the costumes herself for the float our Party entered in the Fourth of July parade.

She threw parties and invited assorted friends from her various paths of life churned them together and waited to see what would happen. She was an irrepressible matchmaker. No sooner would a friend or acquaintance become widowed or divorced than Barbara would find him or her a match, and she would throw a party. Sometimes the matchmaking parties resulted in some rather strange pairings - two people intended by Barbara for different people would unexpectedly wind up together. When Barbara invited a newly divorced girlfriend with a peppy sense of humor who called her ex the Plaintiff, to meet a nice friend of hers, newly widowed who had a yacht at the New Jersey shore, this young woman fell instantly and hard for a disc jockey friend of Dick's who was a hard-drinking, driven and bitten man with more than one former wife. His last wife had fallen down a steep flight of steps and died. When these two met chemistry took over, and the following explosion resulted in a long affair. Although they eventually broke up, I always felt the affair had been good for both of them. He would dedicate songs to her in the early morning hours when the rest of the world was asleep and she never got over the thrill of this. Barbara was to fret and worry over this relationship the entire time it was in progress. Barbara could never understand why this sweet young woman hadn't fallen for the quiet widower she had chosen for her.

Barbara and Dick owned a yacht, and boating was their greatest pleasure. They took Mondays and Fridays off all summer so that they could have four day weekends at the boat. They belonged to a yacht club on the New Jersey shore, and they docked their boat there. Each weekend they would join the other yacht club members for a weekly Saturday night dinner dance preceded by a pre-dinner cocktail party on someone's yacht and an after-dinner dance cocktail party on someone else's boat. This was a hard drinking crew, but they held their liquor well, and they were a generally well-meaning and friendly crowd. Barbara and Dick would frequently have friends to the boat for the weekend. Barbara arranged for my husband and me to take some other couple's three children for the weekend so that they could spend the weekend with Barbara and Dick on their boat. In return it was arranged that this couple would watch our son a few weeks later so that we too could spend a weekend on the yacht.

When we did finally get to go, we enjoyed the weekend although the events seemed a bit strange to me. There were so many cocktails before dinner that we were starved and a bit blotto before we got to have dinner. After dinner there was a dance, and these people, full of booze as they may have been, were able to dance harder and longer than any people I have ever seen. Between the drinking and the dancing, we slept beautifully on the deck of the yacht with the breeze off the water caressing us. The next morning Dick took us all for a sail, and sooner than we would have liked the weekend was over. They took scrupulous care of the boat, and the time spent there and the friends they met at the yacht club were a very important part of their lives. These people made up a large part of the guest list at their parties, and we got to know many of them. I could never keep up with their drinking ability, but they were an amiable bunch.

Barbara was a special friend of the town's most ardent political couple. The woman was affectionately thought of as Pearl Mesta because she hosted many political parties, one in particular around her pool which came to be called the Sip 'N Dip. She and her husband, who looked like Ernest Hemingway in his later bearded years donated gobs of money to the party, and they collected political memorabilia. She could be quite a formidable enemy, as I had learned the many times our political paths had crossed. Once she asked me whether I would like to come and work as a secretary for her husband, who operated a small part-time business in and over the garage. I was heavily involved with politics at the time, so I refused, but did, however, manage to obtain the services of a recently divorced girlfriend of mine who needed a part-time job desperately to supplement her child support payments, which were sparse. Jennifer, the divorced mother, at first enjoyed working there and found him to be the kindest of bosses. However, before her job time there was over, she became involved sexually with him. She then proceeded to blackmail him with threats of telling his wife about their relationship unless he gave her $3,000. He did so, and she quit. I told Barbara about this escapade and about how I had warned Jennifer to be careful with his wife as she could ruin Jennifer if she wanted to. Barbara found the whole affair hilarious and called Martin, the gentleman's name, 'Dirty Marty', and then she volunteered to take the job herself, saying confidently,

"He's known me politically too long to try anything with me."

Barbara was right, and she did enjoy the job, although she and Dick were beginning to tire of politics and life in our suburban town. They were tired of the friendships breaking up every spring when new political sides were drawn. They felt closer ties to their friends at the yacht club, and Dick was soon to be retired so they decided to move to the shore area to be closer to their boat and their boating friends. This move devastated me, but I tried to understand how they felt, and I knew that they were burned out politically, as my husband had long ago burned out politically; and I was nearing the breaking point myself. Strangely, when people who are involved in politics heavily do quit they tend to quit totally and don't even attend the social functions. With the exception of a life-long interest in the elections of the country and their own state, political burn out is a pretty final break with a whole way of life for most of the people who were that involved. Barbara and Dick chose a house that was at the very beginning of the shore area, and therefore close enough to their yacht club activities, but it was also close enough for my husband and me to visit as often as we could wish. I was at that time weaning myself away from a political life by working for a lawyer. Since I was his real estate secretary, Dick and Barbara used my firm for their house closing; and I was handling the paper work. About a month before they were scheduled to move, Barbara went into the hospital to have what she thought was a cyst removed. She was extremely apprehensive, almost fatalistic, about going into the hospital again. We all tried to reassure her with stories of how everyone who had had this operation was doing fine, but she refused to be comforted.

A couple of days following the operation Harry and I went to the hospital as soon as we were allowed to see Barbara. Dick took us out into the hall and told us that the doctors had discovered that Barbara was riddled with cancer, and there was nothing that could be done. We asked whether Barbara had been told, and he answered that she knew. This was a macabre explanation for the horrible backaches that Barbara had been experiencing for a year. She'd been to many doctors, and even to a chiropractor, but no one could tell her why she was suffering so.

Often when we were at her house after dinner, even during parties, Barbara would sit down and cry. It hurt her so. The next few weeks were pretty horrible. We visited Barbara as often as possible when she was in the hospital, but after she got home when I called to ask about visiting her, she replied that she was so weak that she thought she was going to die. She didn't want visitors.

Just at that time our vacation time arrived, and we were on our way to San Francisco for a week — the first time there for both of us, and we were looking forward to it. We hated leaving Barbara, but she was planning to go into the hospital again for a transfusion, which the doctors felt might help with her weakness. We returned on a Saturday late, and on Sunday Harry and I were planning to go to the hospital to see Barbara and give her a stuffed seal we got her in San Francisco because she loved seals. At the last minute I told Harry I was too tired from the trip to go, and could he go without me and tell Barbara I'd see her the next evening during visiting hours. He did go and gave her the seal, but I never did get to see Barbara the following evening. The next night as we were having dinner preparatory to going to the hospital Dick called and said that Barbara had died while he was with her at the dinner hour quite suddenly from a blood clot to the brain.

The shock waves that spread from her death were unbelievable. The next evening we went over to Dick's with some food, and all of us, including Barbara's children, broke down and cried helplessly. The funeral had so many people. Barbara attracted friends effortlessly, and she had political allies as well, so even our Congressman came looking lost and bewildered for a change.

Barbara's candle, however, has not gone out. The flickering flame of her goodness and caring shines in my heart and in the hearts of all who knew her. Her madcap sense of humor and most of all her love remain with us.

Don't Go In The Attic

"Just think," said Aunt Phyllis. "Next week at this time, Susan, you will be in your new house in New Jersey."

Whatever happened in Susan's life from the moment Aunt Phyllis said those words until the long awaited moving day finally arrived remained forever a blur to Susan. Susan was leaving a safe haven of cousins and friends to go to a strange state, new school, and all the attendant horrors and excited anticipations that go along with a change of this magnitude. After an excited flurry of good-byes from Susan's much loved cousins and close friends, the family plus dog were on the road. It was an uneventful trip until they entered the Lincoln tunnel.

"What is that stench?" Susan's father bellowed.

"I don't know," replied Susan's brother, Billy. "Yow: I just stuck my hand in poop. Trinket pooped, and it's all over my hand."

Frantically Billy looked around for something to wipe his offended hand on when his eyes lit on the curly real-haired doll, Sweetie Pie, who was Susan's prize. He then proceeded to wipe his hand on Sweetie Pie's much advertised real-live curly hair. Susan commenced to scream with outrage, and the children were both upset and thrilled by the profanity with which Susan's father reacted to the events of the preceding few minutes. When finally they drove out of the tunnel and were in New Jersey Susan's father pulled up to the side of the road, and he and Susan's mother tried to clean up the mess and soothe the injured feelings of their brood.

After what seemed an eternity the family finally arrived at a beautiful Tudor style house on a serene suburban street facing a strip of almost park-like trees and shrubs. Susan and Billy couldn't wait to get started exploring the house and the surrounding environs. They could make out that only a couple of blocks away was a gorgeous park complete with recreation buildings, and, of course, swings and slides and monkey bars, green baseball and football fields and a brook with a bridge.

Racing through the house, Susan and Billy ran up the wrought iron staircase to the bedrooms. Susan's interest spiked when the two children came upon the den. This wonder of a room was lined with bookshelves bursting with books. Inspecting the books lining the shelves, Susan couldn't contain her delight — the shelves contained the entire sets of Bobbsey Twin books and Nancy Drew. Also there were numerous sets of books about teenage girls and career girls. Billy showed much more interest in a miniature pack of cards he had just unearthed, and he immediately engaged Susan in their favorite game of war. When they finished playing war Billy suggested that they climb the stairs to the attic and see whether there were any treasures to be found there. Nosily they clamored to the staircase which led to the attic just as Susan's father was coming up from downstairs.

"Where are you headed?" he inquired.

"To the attic," Susan said, and they continued up the stairs.

"Don't go in the attic!" Susan's father ordered. "You are never to go in the attic unless your mother and I say you may. Don't disobey me in this," he commanded.

The children were puzzled, but the day held too many delights and forthcoming adventures for them to worry about this strange edict just then. So, the two children went downstairs and outside and went to the park. The park was connected to their grade school and boasted of tennis courts and a backboard. They were informed by some of the neighborhood children that in the winter one of the tennis courts was filled with water and allowed to freeze for ice skating. What an adventure — Susan was expert at roller skating on smooth Brooklyn streets, but ice skating was a marvel as yet untried. When they spied the flag pole Billy asked,

"Does New Jersey have the same flag as we had in Brooklyn?"

"Of course," scoffed Susan, "we're still in the United States, Silly."

"Mother, why can't we go into the attic?" demanded Susan petulantly over dinner.

To the children's surprise their mother didn't immediately go to their side of the argument but instead said,

"Your father has his reasons. Listen to what he said , and obey him."

The incident of the attic was beginning to not only dampen the day but consume Susan with a certain amount of curiosity and some unexplained fear.

"Do you think there's something scary up there, Susan" Billy asked in a quivery voice later when they were alone.

"Nah," Susan said, "Daddy's just being mean. Maybe there's some real neat junk up there that he doesn't want us to touch."

But, she, too, sounded unconvinced. Susan was beginning to think that there were a great many disagreeable things about leaving Brooklyn. She missed her cousins and her best friend, Bubbles — it was a constant ache. However, her mother had promised that next month her cousins would all be over to visit, and that Andy was to stay for a whole week. It was May now, and Susan had just a month to go before the promised treat.

Meanwhile, there was school to contend with. Susan was a friendly soul who was used to being liked. She soon had made quite a few friends, but they all had the puzzling attitude that Brooklyn was a slum and that everyone who lived there lived in a tenement. Susan had never seen a tenement. Susan and Billy were getting their first taste of prejudice, and as always, its flavor was unpleasant.

Sometimes while she lay in bed at night Susan heard strange and ominous sounds coming from the attic. She heard heavy footsteps, bumping, and the whine of a saw. She imagined ghosts and chains, and she questioned Bill about these sounds. Billy, who was a sound sleeper and was not situated as close to the entrance to the attic as Susan was had heard nothing, but Susan's fears seemed to immediately frighten him. For some reason they kept the fears to themselves and didn't question their parents any further about the attic.

Finally it was June. School was out, and the promised visit of her aunt and uncle and cousins was near. Soon they were all spilling out of the car. It was warm enough for a barbecue. After dinner while they were lolling in the yard, Andy gave Susan a scare by thinking she saw a snake wound up high in a tree, but it turned out to be a vine. Huh! Susan hated snakes, and Andy knew this.

The sadness of their leaving was mitigated somewhat because Andy was staying for a whole week. That night when the two girls lay in bed there was a fearful thunderstorm. The lightening was more intense than Susan had ever seen. However thunder storms had always fascinated rather than frightened Susan, and with brave Andy here this was a lark. During a lull in the thunder Susan told Andy about the mystery in the attic.

"Oh, Susan, you are hearing ghosts," Andy warned.

"No." Susan was on the defensive. "I just want to get up there and see what's what."

"The first time we are alone in the house and the circumstances are right you and I will explore the attic. I promise," Andy said.

The ensuing week was one of the most delightful weeks in Susan's memory. The girls spent the gorgeous June week on the screened-in porch having an orgy of reading. They carried arm loads of books from the den to the porch each morning. By evening both girls had read several books each.

True to her promise, as soon as the girls were in the house alone Andy devised a plan. The moment Susan's mother's car had left the driveway the two girls stealthily approached the stairs leading to the attic. As a further precaution Andy made sure Billy was out playing with his friends, and she cautioned Susan not to mention the escapade to him. They crept up the attic stairs only to find when they reached the top that the door to the attic was bolted and locked securely.

"Well, we are temporarily thwarted," Andy mused, "but I'll think of something. Let's look for the key."

However, their search was fruitless and had to be quickly abandoned when Susan's mother returned home unexpectedly. The end of the week came too soon to suit Susan, and Andy departed. Susan continued to search for the key to the attic, but her search was unsuccessful. Susan fell into the summer routine. Actually, it was quite pleasant. Because her parents had been into tournament tennis in their youths, they had encouraged Susan and Bill to learn tennis. Each day Susan headed for the park with her tennis racket and went to the back-board to practice. However, as some of her friends drifted over, the tennis practice ended, and Susan joined her friends in lazing away the summer hours.

The only blight on the summer was the continued noises in the attic at night. It seemed to Susan that the sawing noise and the other noises were more frequent and louder than ever. Finally one rainy Saturday morning the mystery regarding the attic was solved. Susan was sitting on the floor playing with her paper dolls and listening to the radio when she realized that she and Billy might be alone in the house. There was absolute silence from downstairs. Susan tiptoed to the attic staircase and peered up at the door. There was light pouring from the door. She climbed up and discovered that the door was unlocked and unbolted. Billy had followed her up there, and together they entered the dim attic. Susan felt an unpleasant thrill of fear course through her body. The two of them trooped into the attic not knowing what to expect. What to Susan's amazement did she see but the largest and most wonderful doll house she had ever seen or even dreamed of. It was white and green, and it had porches going all around it both upstairs and down. Inside it was furnished and even had electric lights that really worked. It was a Victorian marvel. Inside a family of dolls made to order resided, and in front of the doll house was one of the old cushions from the living room window seats for Susan to kneel upon while playing with the doll house and dolls.

"But, where," Susan gasped, "did it come from?"

From behind her Susan heard her father's voice, "I forgot and left the door unlocked, but we were almost ready for you to see this."

Susan's mother was wearing the look of a cat who had swallowed some cream, and Susan's father said,

It was here when we moved in. The people who used to live here had it custom made for their daughter, but it was too big to take with them when they moved. It was so old that I didn't want you to play with it until I had fixed the wiring and painted and fixed it up. Also it had no dolls, and the ones you already have wouldn't fit, so we had them made to scale.

"Do you like it, Susan?" her father asked.

But there was no need for an answer.

Old Maid

Peg and Mike played games in Mike's bedroom during their childhood when Mike was suffering from asthma attacks. Peg went to his room to visit, and out came the Monopoly, checkers, parcheesi, and, of course, Old Maid. Old Maid was a real favorite. The whimsical pairs the players could make - ballet dancer, magician, artist, clown, witch, rock star, pirate, combined with the more mundane occupations always made Peg think of a circus of characters all upon a stage of the children's making. All the cast were welcome there except for the Old Maid. It was such a simple game; no finer variations or areas for Mike to show off his skill, yet Mike's cunning won out anyway in a more unusual way.

If the children were left to their own devices, the game was played over and over with predictable results. The factor that changed the odds, indeed the whole complexion of the game was when Grandma came to Mike's room to join in the games. She was invariably welcomed with joy by the children as Grandma was not only easy to beat she was naive and suspect able to the children's tricks, most notably Mike's.

"Hi, Mike", Grandma would say. "Shall we play Old Maid today?"

She usually asked for Old Maid because Monopoly was too long, and the other games were too complicated for her to follow. Peg and Mike acquiesced, and the game commenced. Many a spirited game ensued with the colorful professions making pairs all over the bedspread, and the loser was left with the Old Maid to his or her chagrin. Mike, however, didn't like to lose at Old Maid and would go to great lengths to see that this never happened. He would play fiercely for victory, and if all else failed he hid the Old Maid under his pillow. Peg, Mike and Grandma played the game out, but at the end the Old Maid failed to appear in anyone's hand. This always choked Peg up in giggles, as she knew what Mike had done, but Grandma was perpetually confused.

"Where is the Old Maid? How could that have happened? Who is the winner of the game?"

"Grandma," laughed Peg. "Mike has hidden the Old Maid under his pillow again."

"But," protested Grandma. "That's cheating."

Each time Mike hid the Old Maid under his pillow Grandma reacted as though it were the first time. She was incredulous. She had no suspicion at the beginning that it would turn out like this, and unless Mike were losing it — Peg and Grandma took their losing turns at being Old

Maid so that most games were normal. But sometimes when Mike felt that he was losing the game he hid the Old Maid under the pillow, and it was time for the two children to go into spasms of laughter waiting for Grandma to figure out what had happened. Only she never did. Invariably, Grandma threatened not to play Old Maid again the next day, but play again they did as though Mike's trickery had never occurred.

One of the times the trio played Old Maid the luck of the cards was with Mike, and Grandma and Peg kept being the Old Maid. Peg had a trick of her own that she employed during the games. She raised the Old Maid up a little bit so that she would stand out from the rest of her cards, and in that way Peg hoped that Grandma and Mike would pick her. Sometimes it worked, but after a number of games during which Peg employed this trick, Mike caught on.

At the end of this afternoon Mike was stuck with a hand that included the Old Maid. As it looked as though this would be the last game of the afternoon, he was desperate to win, so he did what he usually did he hid the Old Maid under his pillow. The game played out with no ones's having the Old Maid, and Grandma displayed her usual dismay at Mike's deception.

The next day Grandma declared that if Mike didn't play fairly she would never play Old Maid with Peg and Mike again. The three of them had a great deal of fun that day, and the family cat joined them. The large black and white cat, Felix, seemed most interested in the goings on of the Old Maid game. The cat was a fascinated observer of the games. Somehow having the cat present infused the room with a general air of good will. Peggy and Grandma were unusually unlucky, and Peggy's trick of pushing up the Old Maid didn't seem to make anyone pick it out of her hand. Peg and Grandma had many turns of being the Old Maid.

Finally during the last game of the day Mike was stuck with the Old Maid in his hand for a long period. Fearing that no one was going to pluck her from his hand, he resorted to hiding her under his pillow again. The game finished with no Old Maid present. Grandma was dismayed as though it had never happened before.

"Where is the Old Maid?"

"Grandma," Peg said roaring with laughter. "Let's look under Mike's pillow. I'm sure we'll find the Old Maid there as usual." But when they looked there was no Old Maid under the pillow. The children looked everywhere, on the floor and under the bed, but there was no Old Maid that anyone could see. Grandma was really upset this time. Even the usual explanation for the disappearance was not feasible.

"Look!" Peg said "what Felix has in his mouth."

Sure enough the cat was found to be holding the missing Old Maid in her mouth. As Mike could never top that conclusion, he commenced taking normal losing turns at Old Maid from that day on.

Museums

Museums were their hobby - the Metropolitan Museum in New York in particular since they were members. At first their hobby had been New York City where they spent an annual weekend, thus renewing their marriage and their honeymoon joy simultaneously. New York seemed to do all this because they had spent their honeymoon there. However, they progressed from the touristy walks on Broadway, shows on Broadway, and drinks in the glassed-in area of the New York Hilton (on 6th Avenue where they could watch beautifully-dressed people stroll by and get mellow sipping their cocktails at the same time) to museum hopping. They loved the Frick, where they felt as though they were living in an exhaulted atmosphere; the Museum of Modern Art, although Annette liked the abstract paintings better than Nat did; the Guggenheim, where they once saw a spectacular Matisse exhibit, and, of course, the Metropolitan Museum.

Nathan was an amateur Egyptologist and Annette was in love with the Impressionist painters. When the Metropolitan created a space especially for the Impressionist and other Nineteenth-century European paintings, Annette felt as though she would rather be ambling through that section gazing at the Impressionists than anywhere else in the world. In 1993 this area was transformed into the New Nineteenth Century European Paintings and Sculpture Galleries, and they were breathtaking. Nathan and Annette would separate after having Sunday brunch in the museum's restaurant, and he would study the Egyptian section wishing that he had a whole day just to contemplate the museum's Egyptian acquisitions. Meanwhile, Annette after wandering through the Impressionist paintings would stroll through the Twentieth-Century Wing and check out the roof-top sculpture garden should the weather be glorious. After a couple of hours on their own, they would rendezvous in the ever-expanding gift shops of the Metropolitan, which were beginning to resemble a small department store. When Annette gave up smoking, Nathan gifted her with the $100 a month that the cigarettes had cost. With the $100 Annette was able to treat for the expensive brunch and also add to her collection of Metropolitan jewelry, bibelots, scarves, and stationery.

One gorgeous April Sunday morning Annette and Nathan headed for the museum through the rather light for New York traffic not knowing that this particular Sunday was to be adventurous. They enjoyed their usual Sunday brunch, Annette feeling kind of pretty that morning since she'd had her hair frosted the day before making it look blonder than ever, was wearing black to accent the blonde, and her grown son who was visiting that weekend had told her how nice she looked that morning.

"Let's do the Fauve exhibit together, and then we'll part and go our separate routes," suggested Nat.

The Fauves or Wild Beasts were a Post-Impressionist art movement that lasted only approximately four years from 1904 to 1908. As soon as they entered the first of the rooms which housed the collection, Annette knew she was going to be enthralled for the next hour or so. The paintings reminded her of children's colorful crayon drawings. The colors were brilliant, and the use of the color yellow stunned her. Most of the paintings were land or sea-scapes, and the most well-known artist of the group was Matisse, whom Annette had always admired anyway. Overcome by the beauty, Annette paused in the room she had just perused, went to a bench in the center of the room, and perched on the edge of it to catch her visual breath.

"What an unusual necklace you are wearing. What is it?" inquired a good-looking man dressed in a velvet jacket.

"Oh," Annette answered somewhat surprised, "It's a cartouche from Egypt."

She and Nat had been to Egypt and Paris the proceeding Spring, and they had, of course, been to all the museums including the Musee d'Orsay in Paris which housed the Impressionist paintings, thereby putting Annette in heaven for an entire day. She couldn't believe room after room, floor after floor of Impressionist paintings.

"It spells out my name in hieroglyphics."

"It's fascinating," he said and examined it carefully. "Are you with this nice lady?" he asked indicating a friendly-looking woman who happened to be seated next to Annette on the bench.

"No, I'm not with this woman."

"Would you like to see the remainder of the Fauves with me?"

Just as Annette was mouthing the words, "Thank you for asking, but I'm here with my husband," Nathan appeared beside them.

With this the handsome man disappeared rapidly, so fast in fact that Annette couldn't make out where he ended up. She was feeling a glow about what had just transpired when Nat broke in with,

"Good thing I showed up to look for you. He could have turned out to be a serial killer."

"A serial killer?" Annette retorted hurt. "He was gorgeous! And, furthermore, do you really think that the only person who would pick me up would have to be a murderer?"

"You know I didn't mean that. Besides, Ted Bundy was appealing to look at too."

That brought the discussion to a close, and the two split, Annette to the Impressionists as usual and Nathan to the Egyptian section where in one room The Temple of Dendur rescued from the rising waters of the Ashwan Dam and shipped to the Metropolitan in small pieces from Egypt was housed. As she strolled through the air-cooled rooms, which kept the Impressionist paintings intact and free from temperature extremes, Annette mused over what Nat had said. What, she wondered, if instead of thinking me attractive and wanting to spend the afternoon with me he really wanted to murder me or maybe steal my cartouche? As she gazed at her favorite painting—Monet's work of beautifully dressed people by the water on a meltingly gorgeous Spring morning, she suddenly felt cold all over.

She began to tremble and to have what could only have been termed a panic attack. She managed to get to the bench in the middle of the room with the Van Gogh paintings and sat there trying to catch her breath.

No, she thought, Nat is abnormally jealous, although he pretends to not a shred of jealousy, and he just said that to prick my rapidly-filling balloon. She sat there for several minutes thinking related calming thoughts and then got up and resumed her browsing. Occasionally if the thoughts reoccurred about the man who had tried to pick her up being a mass murderer she would either sit down or wander over to the nearest display selling jewelry or prints or both, and the thought of buying any of the displayed treasures settled her nerves and put her once again in her good museum — going mood.

That particular Sunday Annette felt particularly revved up (probably because of the proceeding events), and she managed to see all of the Impressionist Wing and all three floors of the Twentieth-Century Wing, a well-appointed section of the museum donated by Lila Acheson Wallace. Annette felt that if one had to die eventually, to live on in the form of endowing a museum would be one of the best ways. After all her looking Annette went up to the outdoor sculpture garden where she and Nat had planned to meet. Nat was late, and Annette passed the time sitting on a bench and enjoying the pulchritude of both the sculpture and the New York City skyline from the rooftop. Most of the sculpture was Rodin s, and seeing his massive but graceful figures reminded Annette of their trip to the Rodin Museum when in Paris. It was late April, but surrounding the museum were early-blooming roses and lilacs, although neither flower had begun to bloom back in

New Jersey. The lawn of the front of the Rodin Museum had "The Thinker", and Annette had a picture that Nathan snapped of her in front of him. The inside of the museum was elegant and naturally housed many of Rodin's best works including the white marble "The Kiss" of which Annette bought a note card in the gift shop. She would have liked a reproduction of that particular piece, but the prices of the reproductions were astronomical as were most of the prices of Paris. After seeing the inside of the museum and taking Annette's picture on the front lawn in front of The Thinker, the two of them wandered to the back of the museum and couldn't believe what they saw. There was a small but long pond surrounded by flowers and hedges. Sculpture abounded, and almost hidden in the shrubbery was an outdoor terrace restaurant where they stopped and had a French pastry and café au lait. Visiting the Rodin Museum in Paris was an experience to draw on in later years.

"Sorry I'm late," Nathan tossed off as he greeted Annette, "but I had the strangest experience."

Annette, who always wanted to hear stories in great detail although Nat always told them sparsely, asked him to relate his experience leaving nothing out.

"I was looking at the Egyptian books in the gift shop and . . ."

"Why were you in the gift shop now? We usually do it last," Annette wondered aloud.

"I suddenly remembered that the last time we were here they were supposed to reserve something for me, and I didn't want to wait and possibly forget to ask about it."

"Anyway, what happened?" Annette was getting slightly impatient.

"A lovely young girl approached me and asked me about the books. She is studying Egypt in college and is interested in going on a dig. We got into a long involved conversation about Egypt."

"Oh, how nice," Annette murmured. "I bet she wanted you to pick her up."

"Yes," Nat remarked. "Actually I think she did."

"Notice I didn't call her a hatchet murderess or the, woman from Fatal Attraction," Annette couldn't resist saying.

Since Nathan didn't reply to this sally, Annette switched the subject. "Remember in Breakfast at Tiffany's where Audrey Hepburn as Holly says that if she has a case of the mean reds, a condition much more serious than the blues, she just walks through Tiffany's and feels calm?"

"Sure," Nat said.

"Well, that's the way I feel here at the museum. As if, as Holly said, nothing bad could ever happen to you here. If that guy were a murderer I can't believe he would choose the Metropolitan to do his stalking. Remember that movie where the two small children hid out in the Metropolitan for a week or so without being caught? They were only children, and they weren't even harmed. In fact, their sojourn at the Met ended up solving all their problems."

"Let's go to the gift shop. My book perusing was interrupted, and I bet you can't wait to add to your jewelry collection." Annette loved the Metropolitan jewelry so much that each day she would decide which Metropolitan pin or earrings to put on.

They spent the next 45 minutes or so shopping and felt that it was time to go home since parking in the museum's garage although cheaper than in the rest of the city was still dear enough to curtail the number of hours they could have spent if they didn't have to consider it.

"I have an unusual idea," Annette mused. "Could we possibly sit in the area at the front of the restaurant and have a glass of wine before we leave?"

"Why not? We're probably into the next parking hour anyway," Nat replied.

After a few hours of touring the museum, sitting down was a pleasure. As always, just as Annette and Nathan were ready to leave, the museum had filled up to the point of being crowded. On rainy days especially the native New Yorkers would invade the museum sometime after having had their late brunches at home or at some restaurant other than the museum's. The little table at which they were sitting to have their wine was one of a small bunch of round tables especially put there close to the bar for that purpose. On Friday and Saturday evenings most of the dim lighting was furnished by candles on these tables and the tables in the restaurant. On the second floor little tables were set up for wine drinking while violins played chamber music, and in the restaurant on the first floor there was a pianist playing show tunes.

"Well, although we have visited the museums in Paris, Egypt, London, Italy, and many cities in the United States this remains the best," Annette burbled.

"We've also used all the rest rooms in museums all over three continents," Nat joked.

"Yes," recalled Annette, "and in the Cairo Museum rest room as you walk in the matron hands you exactly two squares of toilet paper. Lord knows what you would do if you should need more."

After about a half hour of sipping their glasses of wine, Annette and Nat got ready to leave-reluctantly as usual. As they were gathering their parcels and leaving the table they made way for the next occupants. The couple approaching their table to sit down in the seats they had just vacated was constructed of the man in the velvet jacket and the college girl who was interested in Egypt. The four looked at each other, and everyone smiled, although each for a separate reason.

A Vaudeville Team

To begin with, the name of the firm sounded like an Irish Vaudeville team-Delaney, Delaney, and O'Sullivan. Ellen's first impression was one of elegant blueness. The law office was tastefully decorated, and behind the receptionist's desk sat an elderly blonde woman who was introduced to Ellen as Miss Jones. Miss Jones upon standing revealed herself to be slightly crippled probably from polio. She proceeded to stammer out an apology for the lateness of Hannah, the woman who was to interview Ellen, when out of a huge office to the left came a young, handsome and extremely polite man. He introduced himself to Ellen as Terry Delaney and said that he would conduct the interview himself.

On the way to the conference room where the interview was to be held, Mr. Delaney pointed out a small but beautiful office which seemed to have been converted from the old law library as important looking books lined all the shelves. It had a desk that looked as though it belonged in the study of an old but regal house.

"This," said Terry, "would be your office should you be my secretary."

From that moment Ellen knew she just had to have that job. Ellen had interesting but strange credentials, and happily, they struck just the right note with Terry Delaney. Ellen had worked for the last seven years as the Republican Executive Secretary for the Essex County Republican Committee. She had helped to shape, mold, and elect people to Republican power positions from local councilmen to State Senate and even President. Also on her resume was Councilman's wife, since her husband had been a Republican councilman in Maplewood, the borough where Ellen lived. Unknown to Ellen, Terry Delaney was a snob, and the idea of hiring a secretary who had been so heavily involved in the political arena appealed to him.

On the wall in the conference room was a portrait of a dour but distinguished man which dominated the entire room. Ellen later learned that this was Wilbert P. Delaney, Sr., who was recently deceased but whose name was still listed on the letterhead indicating that the gentleman was deceased. Just as this part of the interview was winding down, the bathroom door slammed and out sauntered Miss Jones ambling down the corridor with a stream of toilet paper protruding from her slacks.

After Ellen passed a typing test with flying colors, Terry Delaney said that he would call her no later than the next morning, and Ellen walked down the long hall preparing to exit. Watching her departure were at least seven pairs of eyes. She cut a nice enough picture with her long black hair, brown eyes, well-cut clothes, shapely ankles, and chubby figure.

On her first morning on the new job Ellen met the other members of the law firm and the secretaries who were employed there. As the name indicated, this was a family law firm and included Terry Delaney, his brother Will Delaney, and their brother- in-law Barry O'Sullivan. The three men were thirty-something and exceedingly good looking, especially Barry O'Sullivan who was black Irish in his looks with black hair and blue eyes. His vocabulary was superb, and taking his dictation any secretary would need to sit on her dictionary. Not part of the firm, but definitely the steel backbone behind it was the matriarch of the family, the boys' mother, Kathleen Delaney. She and the two unmarried boys lived in a huge house in South Orange with their housekeeper, the ever faithful Colleen. Ellen was instructed firmly not to ask Miss Jones for help, as she was elderly and was becoming senile. Instead Ellen was advised to seek help from Mary Jo, the slender, beautiful secretary for Will Delaney or Hannah, Barry O'Sullivan's efficient secretary. Hannah was a married old maid. Extremely prim and prissy, she nevertheless did a top notch job for the demanding Barry O'Sullivan.

At lunchtime that first day Ellen met the last person to make up the menagerie of her new work life - Jean. Jean worked in an office across the hall, and when the door to that office opened torrents of smoke came pouring out of the messiest office Ellen had ever seen in her life. Emerging from the chaos was a pretty, albeit sloppy young woman. Jean had once worked for Delaney, Delaney, and O'Sullivan but now worked for her father. She spent her days reading Harlequin romance novels and answering the telephone. Her story of why she left Delaney, Delaney, and O'Sullivan was enough to raise the hairs on Ellen's head.

While Miss Jones may not have been the person to go to with a work related problem, she was a font of information on the whole Delaney clan. She had worked for old Mr. Delaney even before the boys were born, and therefore, she contained a treasure chest of knowledge of their background.

"Don't mind Terry's temper tantrums," she whispered sotto voce to Ellen. "He's been to a psychiatrist you know."

According to Miss Jones, Terry's problems arose because Colleen, the housekeeper, spilled hot chicken soup on him when he was a baby. As for Will Delaney, according to Miss Jones he was in love with a girl of Italian background, who was an advertising executive with a New York firm. Apparently, Will couldn't marry this woman because Kathleen Delaney disapproved heartily. There was even folk lore regarding the handsome Barry O'Sullivan. After a dissolute youth drinking and carousing, he made a vow to himself never to have another drink and had kept the vow until this day. Another interesting tidbit was about Barry's father who had become a Priest after his wife died and when his children were grown. Miss Jones reluctantly concluded her recitation of family quirks by saying that old Wilbert P. Delaney, Sr., whom Ellen figured she had had a crush on, was a neurotic who was afraid to drive his car over bridges of any type.

Ellen swiftly learned that in addition to her specified duties like answering all the telephone calls, typing wills and legal agreements and handling the real estate closings; 90% of her duties would be to listen to Terry Delaney's problems. The reason she had her private office was so Terry could retreat there and tell Ellen his troubles. Ellen was sympathetic and, according to Terry, motherly, and she became the perfect receptacle for his extraordinary recitals. Ellen and Terry had been born within a month of each other, and therefore, had many similar friends and acquaintances (they had grown up in the same town). Ellen had dated boys from the Hun School, the prep school that Terry had attended, and they both graduated the same year.

As time passed Ellen and Terry found themselves in a husband and wife office relationship. Terry was the soul of politeness in public, but he was extremely rude and fussy in his role as boss. He was prone to temper tantrums, and Ellen had to adjust to his ways or lose her self-confidence completely. Part of the problem was that Terry was a procrastinator. For most of the day, and for that matter week, Terry would put off his clients and his entire work load, opting instead for several gab fest with Ellen. Then at 4:00 p.m. every day, especially Friday afternoons, Terry would go into a flurry of activity frequently causing Ellen to stay on in the office until nearly six every day.

Life at the office settled into its own routine. The daily schedule was frequently punctuated by visits from the matriarch herself, Kathleen Delaney, always accompanied by the omnipresent Colleen. Ellen was quite nervous indeed the first day she met Mrs. Delaney who was an elegant woman of seventy who went to Mass every morning and included at least one Priest among her regular dinner guests. She knew the workings of the office inside and out, and Terry was always sure to answer at least some of his phone calls when Mother was present. Hannah, Barry's secretary, was prone to sudden angers about nothing at all, and often included in the tempest was Jean from across the hall. Going their own ways and causing barely a ripple in the office proceedings were Will Delaney and his secretary, Mary Jo. Mary Jo was a jewel. Not only was she about the best secretary Ellen had ever encountered, she was friendly and ever helpful to Ellen.

Miss Jones was a case history all by herself. She absolutely lived for the firm, and her loyalty was unquestioned. But whether due to her age, high blood pressure or some other factor, she was the most incompetent secretary Ellen had ever seen. She would never write down telephone messages, but instead insisted that she never forgot a message. As a result there were frequent explosions when court dates got mixed up and other important business neglected due to her negligence. Since she never answered the telephone unless Ellen was on another line, this confusion resulted almost every time she handled a call. Once after Miss Jones had gone home, Will Delaney showed Ellen a letter that she had given to him to sign and mail out. She had neglected to put in the salutation so this particular letter had no 'Dear John' or anyone else for that matter. All in all there was a real circus atmosphere around the firm. Miss Jones rarely went home. She worked until seven each evening except Friday afternoons when she had a hairdresser appointment, and she would close all the cabinets and lock the files before anyone else was ready to leave.

It soon became Ellen's number one priority to get the two Delaney boys married. Ellen had been happily married for twenty years, and she couldn't believe that both of the Delaney men were bachelors in their thirties. Barry O'Sullivan was married to the beautiful Marie, Will and Terry's youngest sister, and they had three lovely children. So he at least was not in Ellen's plans to play cupid. She heartily felt that Will should marry Anna, the attractive advertising executive, in spite of Mrs. Delaney and the threat of losing his inheritance. Each month Richard became sadder as more and more of his bachelor cronies took to the altar. As for Terry, Ellen had a plan there, too. There was a young, pretty heiress whose legal business Terry was tending called Margaret Van Allen. This Margaret called Meg had a crush on Terry, and she was rather obvious about it. She sent him effusive postcards from Europe and set up numerous unnecessary office visits with Terry. However, Terry was soon to unveil a strange fantasy to Ellen which was sure to botch thoroughly any of Ellen's matchmaking plans. Terry's fantasy was almost an aberration, or so it seemed to Ellen.

One beautiful Friday afternoon in May Terry came to Ellen's office to talk about his weekend plans. The Delaney family owned a house at the New Jersey shore, to which the whole clan retreated each Friday and returned on Monday morning.

"Ellen, I can't decide what to wear tonight. Please give me some advice," implored Terry.

Ever hopeful, Ellen inquired as to whether Terry had a date.

"Not exactly a date, but I am meeting some people at a disco tonight, and I want to look handsome and twenty-five," Terry replied.

"The handsome part is easy," Ellen replied truthfully, "and if you really want to look twenty-five wear jeans."

"No, Ellen, I want the preppie look."

"What's going on?"

"If I let you in on this you must promise to keep it a secret from the rest of the family," Terry said, and proceeded to tell Ellen the most fantastic story.

As his tale evolved it appeared as though Terry had met a group of young people in their twenties in a neighboring, but not nearly so swanky as his own, shore town. As Ellen gently probed she found that the source of his keen interest was a young blonde girl who was living with a young man. The woman in question was to go nameless, but Terry described her as looking like Cathy Lee Crosby. Terry had actually been invited to a couple of parties this group had hosted, but the hub of activity for these people, during the day at least, was a coffee shop where the blonde worked as a waitress. Here at the coffee shop, which Terry haunted, everyone met and made their plans. The group were what is known as 'townies', as they lived at the shore year round, and were in Terry's opinion, definitely a couple of notches below him socially. Instead of telling these people the truth about himself, Terry had told them that he was a rising young attorney at a large New York law firm. He was also using an assumed name. Ellen tried to warn Terry that the girl was attached since she was living with someone and apparently had been for some time. However, Terry, undaunted in his quest for romance, went faithfully to the shore every weekend until December.

As Christmas approached, he had the idea of bringing the group, in care of the girl, a couple of bottles of good champagne as his Christmas offering. Ellen was amazed to find that he really carried through the rather courtly gesture. As time went on Terry's obsession grew rather than diminished. He spent an hour each Friday deciding what to wear for the weekend. Although Ellen continued to urge him to wear jeans, even designer jeans if he couldn't stoop so low as to wear Lees or Levis, he continued to wear outfits like expensive corduroy pants with green ducks imprinted on them with matching sweaters.

Here a word must be said about Terry's wardrobe. He had custom made shirts and suits. He had ties and shirts and tennis outfits still in boxes at home. He had fourteen caret gold cuff links. It was all Ellen could do to keep herself from ripping off his clothes for her husband, Larry, to wear. During the Christmas season in question, Terry wore a tie that was rather special - it had little people imprinted on it.

"Who are those little people on your tie?" Ellen asked.

"Shoppers, Ellen," Terry answered.

Sure enough, all the people on the tie were carrying packages. The implications of a wardrobe so vast that it included such a tie staggered Ellen's imagination.

Ellen began to get frightened for Terry when she learned that he had placed himself as a sentinel across the street from the girl's apartment and would spend hours just trying to look into her windows. Ellen was scared because of the degree into which Terry had immersed himself with the life of this girl.

Vying for attention along with the group at the shore was the problem of Terry's long time friend Mark James. This Mark James and Terry had gone to law school together, and they had a competition going. One day around Christmas time a card came for Terry from Mark stating that he had been made a partner in a prestigious law firm. This put Terry in the throes of jealousy. He dictated a congratulatory note to Ellen at least five times and rejected each copy Ellen handed to him. Finally the correct note was struck, and the letter went off. Terry put Ellen to work looking up Mark's number, and finally telephone contact was established between the two men. Ellen knew enough to be very friendly but businesslike with Mark's secretary, who Terry assumed would have to be the most efficient secretary ever born if she worked for Mark. Finally, a luncheon date was set up between the two lawyers.

Mark was scheduled to meet Terry at Terry's office on a Friday at noon. The office was in a flurry — windows washed, furniture polished, and, of course, everyone dressed in his or her best. Ellen had on a white wool dress and a green velvet jacket. Terry was dressed as if to go yachting in a navy blazer adorned with gold buttons and white duck trousers. When the fatal hour arrived Terry was so paralyzed with fear that he hid in Barry's office down the hall leaving Barry to entertain Mark while Miss Jones and Ellen tried to persuade Terry to come and meet his guest. After an hour of this nonsense Terry finally emerged from Barry's office and greeted his guest with apologies for being tied up in a meeting with a client. Ellen supposed that the luncheon went okay except that Mark revealed that he ran every year in the New York Marathon. This was a sore point with Terry because he went every week to the New York Athletic Club to run around the track for a few times and then dine in their excellent dining room. In Terry's opinion Mark must be in superior condition to compete in the New York Marathon, and he sulked.

Weekends with the mystery girl continued with Terry's obsession becoming greater. Terry spent a month trying to decide what kind of tee shirt to give the girl as a surprise present. He finally decided to give her and her lover matching tee shirts with "Don't touch me I'm living with someone" on them. For three weeks he brought the tee shirts to the shore on weekends, but he always chickened out and brought them back home again. Finally a month after he bought the shirts he left them with the girl at the coffee shop and ran out without waiting for her reaction.

He continued to haunt her street and try to see into her house, and this made Ellen very nervous. One fateful Monday morning when Ellen arrived at work everything was in an uproar. She was greeted in the hall by Hannah who said "I can't believe I work in a place that has people like this. I'm so ashamed:"

Puzzled, Ellen went to Mary Jo's office before going to her own. Mary Jo said that Terry had been arrested on Saturday for being a Peeping Tom. Barry had had to bail him out of jail and was planning to defend him, as Barry was the best criminal lawyer in the firm. Terry was in a weird mood, even more so than usual. Mama was on the scene, and Will was as grumpy as a bear.

"Ellen," Terry said, "can you imagine arresting me just for looking in her window?"

"But," Ellen stammered, "looking in her window is being a Peeping Tom."

"I can't believe that she is pressing charges when we have been friends for so long, and I gave her the champagne and tee shirts and all."

"Well," Ellen said, "maybe she is a little frightened and doesn't know what else to do."

The day continued in a turmoil. Barry and Will closeted themselves in Barry's office to discuss the defense. Terry alternately pouted or fretted and paced, and Miss Jones was so distraught that her work was more disorganized than usual, and the few phone calls that she took were totally messed up. Terry was afraid of his day in Court. One of Terry's quirks was that he was afraid to go into Court to defend his clients. He was always saying that this time he would do it, but on the day before the trial began he would hand over the case to Barry or Will. Once Terry had been appointed public defender to a man who was accused of stealing quarters from the parking meters in town. He'd been found with dozens of quarters, and a powder test showed that he had broken into the machines. The most Terry was hoping to do was to keep him out of jail until after Christmas. The day before the case was due to go to trial Terry asked Will to take it over for him. Will was livid.

"I've never even met the man, and you're only giving me one day to prepare the case," he protested.

However, as usual, he bailed Terry out and took the case.

Now Terry was to have his day in Court, and he was to be the defendant. Ellen and Mary Jo tried to be as calm and sympathetic as possible, but he continued to rave and rant. Barry and Will were working on getting the girl to drop the charges. If somehow they could settle out of court it would solve everyone's problems. Terry was threatening not to show up in Court.

"You have to," Ellen protested, "you're the defendant."

Terry was rapidly becoming a basket case. His trips to the shore ceased, and with this development came foul humor. He literally became a monster to work for, and everyone else was so out of sorts that the office became a place Ellen dreaded to enter in the mornings. Terry planned a trip to Florida for the time of the Court date, but he didn't have the nerve to actually go and break his bail agreement.

The day before the trial dawned, and everyone's nerves were shot. Barry and Will were planning a last ditch effort to get the girl to drop the charges or settle out of Court, and Terry was fuming. Finally at 4 p.m. Barry swept into Ellen's office where Terry was sitting in abject despair and announced,

"We've done it: The girl is willing to drop the charges on the condition that you never enter the town again." She never wants to see hair nor hide of you or the Mercedes again."

Barry was triumphant, but Terry seemed as dejected as before. He quietly told Barry that he would agree to her terms, and Barry departed. Terry then began his litany.

"Can you believe how she has betrayed me?" he wailed. He actually seemed to feel as though he had been cheated or otherwise injured.

"You have a whole life apart from that girl," Ellen comforted. "You could try to be sensible and do some interesting things with your own crowd."

But Terry wasn't to be consoled. "It turns out that John, the school teacher in the crowd who first took me to parties and introduced me around is an alcoholic. I can't believe my luck in choosing friends. The whole crowd turns out to be rotten, Ellen. Can you imagine it?"

Things around the office gradually went back to what passed around here as normal, and Terry even began to go back to the shore. However, he went nowhere near the town where his lady love lived. One beautiful, sunny Friday afternoon Ellen was working on closing papers for a bank when Terry appeared in her office quite elated.

"Meg is going to a country club dance with me," he announced jubilantly.

Ellen was delighted. "This," she said, "is what I've been hoping for you all along since the first day I got here."

"I know," Terry answered. "That's why you are the first person to know."

Ellen felt vindicated. Although she had not delivered a marriage for either brother, a start had been made. Terry was actually starting to date for the first time in his life. Ellen envisioned many Friday afternoons advising Terry on his romance, and Ellen felt fulfilled.

Try Outs

Sitting in the back of Mr. Deeds' Creative Writing and Dramatics classroom, Rachel surveyed the competition as she both dreaded and anticipated the try outs for this year's All School production of Brigadoon. Although one of the school's finest actresses, Rachel had never been in an All School show because they were always musicals to give a larger number of the students a chance to appear in them. Rachel could neither sing nor dance, and the musicals seldom called for non-singing or non-dancing parts. Brigadoon was an exception — the show featured the coveted non-singing part of Jane Ashton who gets left behind in New York by Tommy Albright, the hero. She's the girl Tommy eventually jilts. Rachel felt as though she had a chance because Mr. Deeds, the director, had directed her in Dramatic Club shows and was familiar with her work.

Here came Mr. Deeds and upon his entrance the try outs began. Rachel read flawlessly — she seemed to be on a roll. Each time it was her turn to read the part her reading outshone the rest. These preliminary try outs were being held on a Friday afternoon with the final try outs to be held on Monday afternoon.

"Rachel," Mr. Deeds said after the try outs wound down, "you gave a competent reading today. I have to talk with Mr. Kaufmant the musical director, but there's a good chance you may get this part."

Mr. Kaufman didn't know Rachel since she was not usually in the chorus. Once in Junior High she had sung in a pageant, but this year, her sophomore year in high school, was a long way away from her one and only dealing with Mr. Kaufman.

The weekend passed in a blur for Rachel. She was completely focused on the Monday try outs and the long awaited chance to be in that All School Show. Monday afternoon Rachel galloped toward the auditorium and almost charged into Charlie her boyfriend of the season. Charlie attended a private school, and his appearance here bewildered and flustered Rachel.

"Charlie, what ... how did you get here, and on a Monday. Were you expelled?"

"No, just suspended for a week for smoking. My Mom is freaking. I cut out and came to find you. Let's go for a coke."

Rachel met Charlie during Christmas break when he was home on vacation. She and a group of her friends were returning from a caroling party and were rosy and red-cheeked from the cold and wrapped in their colorful woolen scarfs and mittens when they bumped into him. Rachel knew that Charlie had dated Phyllis, the head twirler and drum majorette, and had heard rumors that each time he and Phyllis broke up he dated Phyllis look-a-likes. Phyllis had black hair and snapping black eyes fringed with long eyelashes, and Rachel fell into this category as did Maryann, a close friend of Rachel's whom he had already dated although it wasn't serious for either of them, and they were still friends. Rachel looked extra attractive that evening as she had dressed for the party. At the party she flirted and had been flirted with so she was in the correct mode to banter with Charlie. They clicked within fifteen minutes and by the end of the evening they were going together although whether for just a couple of dates or a relationship would have to be determined.

At the present time Rachel hoped that Charlie might bestow his I.D. bracelet on her as he had done sometime back with the omnipresent Phyllis. However, today Charlie was an unwelcome distraction. His presence put her mind in a turmoil blending her romantic feelings with her nervous and focused efforts regarding the try outs.

"Charlie, I can't go for a coke or anywhere. Final try outs for the All School show are this afternoon, and I have a good chance for a part."

Since Charlie was in private school, he had never seen her act nor had he known her long or well enough to be mindful of her passion for acting.

"I'll go with you, and after we'll go downtown."

Thus they approached the auditorium hand in hand, and the atmosphere was charged with tension. Rachel's almost pure concentration on the part snapped, and she felt at sea.

When they approached the auditorium Mr. Deeds saw her and walked over to hold a conference with Mr. Kaufman to talk about her Rachel suspected. This only increased her now unpleasant agitation. Before she could catch her breath, Mr. Deeds handed her a script and asked her to come on the stage and read. Charlie smiled encouragement, and Rachel climbed the steps to the stage with her legs and feet wobbling. All she could see and all she was aware of was Charlie's watching her. She barely glanced at the script and proceeded to read. In her haste she misread the scene, and consequently gave the reading an incorrect inflection and interpretation.

Midway into the reading Rachel realized her error, but by then she was being asked to stop. It was over. Although she was asked to read for Meg, one of the minor singing parts, she knew that she had botched her one chance to fulfill a dream years in the making. To add a extra dose of misery to the caldron of woe she was stirring, Charlie said,

"You're not much of an actress. Maybe you should do something else, paint scenery or something." The unfairness of this coming from someone who had not only caused this upset, but who had never seen her act.

Rachel decided to be a pragmatist and be glad that Charlie was here for the week, and so they started for town and the coke he had mentioned. Rachel struggled with yet another dilemma because now Charlie would be here on Friday night, and not expecting him home she had another date. Maryann was infatuated with a shy boy named Hank who wouldn't date her unless his best friend, Bob, were along. Thinking that Charlie was unavailable, Rachel had promised to go although she didn't like Bob. Now she haltingly told Charlie who didn't react well.

The week continued in this unpleasant fashion. As Rachel had feared, she didn't get the part of Jane. As she couldn't be in the chorus, this left her as a hostess the night of the All School Show ushering people to their seats. Friday came and Charlie told her that he'd go to the basketball game and see her the next night at a dance they were attending. He called her Saturday morning at Maryann's where she was spending the night.

"Rachel, wear your yellow chiffon like you did at the first dance we went to."

She agreed and unsuspectingly went to the dance and spent most of the evening with Charlie. He returned to private school on Sunday, and she went to school on Monday expecting to see him again on his next weekend home. At ten o'clock that morning in the ladies room she saw Phyllis who was surrounded by a giggling group of girls.

"Oh, Phyllis," one of them squealed, "when did Charlie give it to you?"

Rachel peered at Phyllis's arm, and there was Charlie's I.D. bracelet the same one she had been praying for.

"Friday night," Phyllis said.

Friday night. This meant that all of Saturday had been a sham and that Charlie presented his bracelet to Phyllis on Friday evening at the basketball game. Rachel learned a bitter lesson from all of this. Charlie was just trying her and her other dark-haired friends out. They were all try outs for the real event — Phyllis. Rachel let her romantic feelings for Charlie get in the way of her achieving the goal she had set for herself of landing that part. Never again would she let something trivial, as this turned out to be, get in the way of what was paramount. Maybe the part was a minor price to pay to discover a truth of this magnitude. She felt older and smarter that day than she had ever felt before.

About The Author

Susan C. Barto was *born* on the beautiful day of June 21, 1941. The beloved child of Eda and Wiliam Forcellon. As she grew up she met a terrific man (Harry W. Barto) who later became her loving husband. Later Susan gave birth to a handsome baby boy (William M. Barto).

Susan's *educational* background was develped at Katherine Gibbs School and Union College, NJ. She has traveled extensively to Egypt, Italy, England and France.

She has experience with two years Legal Secretary - Legislative Aide; A writer for the last ten years. Her *memberships* include President Friends of the Hunterdon Museum of Art — New Providence Library Board, NJ — Raritan Valley College Book Group.

Susan Barto's *honors* are: Golden Certificate Award, Drury's Publishing™ — Plaque from Library Board, Listed in 1999-2000 Who's Who In The East and 2000 Who's Who In America, and Who's Who In Literary Achievement.

Her *publishing credits* include eleven stories published with Creative With Words, One story published with Yesterday's Magazette, One story published with Writer's Guidelines and News, One story published with Good Old Days, and several stories published with Drury's Publishing™, along with four books of stories published by Drury's Publishing™.

On a more *personal note* Susan C. Barto says: ***"I love to write. Writing defines who I am."***